I Was Walking Down the Road

I Was Walking Down the Road

by Sarah E. Barchas

pictures by Jack Kent

SCHOLASTIC INC.
New York Toronto London Auckland Sydney

This book belongs to

___

ISBN 0-590-10137-4

24 23 8 9/9 0 1 2/0

Printed in the U.S.A.

For my parents

I was walking down the road.
Then I saw a little toad.

I caught it.
I picked it up.

I put it in a cage.

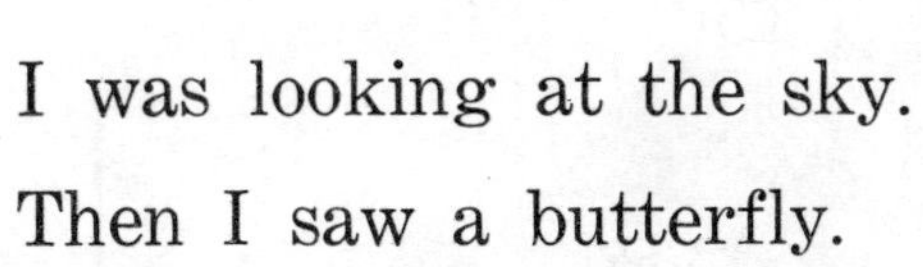

I was looking at the sky.
Then I saw a butterfly.

I caught it.

I picked it up.

I put it in a cage.

I was working with a rake.

Then I saw a little snake.

I caught it.

I picked it up.

I put it in a cage.

I was jumping on a log.

Then I saw a little frog.

I caught it.

I picked it up.

I put it in a cage.

I was cleaning up the rug.
Then I saw a little bug.

I caught it.

I picked it up.

I put it in a cage.

I was waiting for the mail.

Then I saw a little snail.

I caught it.

I picked it up.

I put it in a cage.

I was sweeping up the house.

Then I saw a little mouse.

I caught it.

I picked it up.
I put it in a cage.

I was looking for my mitten.

Then I found a little kitten.

I caught it.

I picked it up.

I put it in a cage.

I was eating cake and cider.
Then I saw a little spider.

I caught it.

I picked it up.

I put it in a cage.

I was reading something funny.

Then I saw a little bunny.

I caught it.

I picked it up.

I put it in a cage.

I was pushing a wheelbarrow.

Then I saw a little sparrow.

I caught it.

I picked it up.

I put it in a cage.

I was looking at my pets.
Then I saw them look at me.

I sat a while.
I thought a while.
And then . . .

I set them free.